P9-CEE-621

TO

FROM

This book is dedicated to the gift
my true love gave to me,
my son, Ian Maxwell Radzinski

Text copyright © 1992 by Chronicle Books
Illustrations copyright © 1992 by Kandy Radzinski
All Rights reserved.
Book designed by Karen Pike
Type composition by   Typecast, Inc.
Printed in Singapore.

ISBN 0-8118-0102-0
CIP Data available

Distributed in Canada by Raincoast Books
8680 Cambie Street, Vancouver B.C. V6P 6M9
10 9 8 7 6 5 4

Chronicle Books
275 Fifth Street
San Francisco, California 94103

THE
TWELVE CATS
OF
CHRISTMAS

Kandy Radzinski

Chronicle Books San Francisco

On the first day of Christmas,
my true love gave to me
a white cat with a red bow.

On the second day of Christmas,
my true love gave to me
two cats asleep,
and a white cat with a red bow.

On the third day of Christmas,
my true love gave to me
three climbing cats,
two cats asleep,
and a white cat with a red bow.

On the fourth day of Christmas,
my true love gave to me
four Siamese,
three climbing cats,
two cats asleep,
and a white cat with a red bow.

On the fifth day of Christmas,
my true love gave to me
five golden cats,
four Siamese,
three climbing cats,
two cats asleep,
and a white cat with a red bow.

On the sixth day of Christmas,
my true love gave to me
six cats a-playing,
five golden cats,
four Siamese,
three climbing cats,
two cats asleep,
and a white cat with a red bow.

On the seventh day of Christmas,
my true love gave to me
seven cats a-gazing,
six cats a-playing,
five golden cats,
four Siamese,
three climbing cats,
two cats asleep,
and a white cat with a red bow.

On the eighth day of Christmas,
my true love gave to me
eight cats a-lapping,
seven cats a-gazing,
six cats a-playing,
five golden cats,
four Siamese,
three climbing cats,
two cats asleep,
and a white cat with a red bow.

On the ninth day of Christmas,
my true love gave to me
nine cats a-hiding,
eight cats a-lapping,
seven cats a-gazing,
six cats a-playing,
five golden cats,
four Siamese,
three climbing cats,
two cats asleep,
and a white cat with a red bow.

On the tenth day of Christmas,
my true love gave to me
ten cats a-hunting,
nine cats a-hiding,
eight cats a-lapping,
seven cats a-gazing,
six cats a-playing,
five golden cats,
four Siamese,
three climbing cats,
two cats asleep,
and a white cat with a red bow.

On the eleventh day of Christmas,
my true love gave to me
eleven cats a-racing,
ten cats a-hunting,
nine cats a-hiding,
eight cats a-lapping,
seven cats a-gazing,
six cats a-playing,
five golden cats,
four Siamese,
three climbing cats,
two cats asleep,
and a white cat with a red bow.

On the twelfth day of Christmas,
my true love gave to me
twelve cats a-leaping,
eleven cats a-racing,
ten cats a-hunting,
nine cats a-hiding,
eight cats a-lapping,
seven cats a-gazing,
six cats a-playing,
five golden cats,
four Siamese,
three climbing cats,
two cats asleep,
and a white cat with a red bow.